To Our Badger Family...
PEACE !
Siiji and Mary
2007

Sunny and Wondrous Cat Cousins

Mary Hochenauer & Lois (Suji) Hochenauer-Fox
Illustrated by Diane Lucas

Gnatcatcher Children's Books

Our vision is . . .

To help create a world where everyone resolves conflicts fairly and peacefully

We dedicate this book to . . .

Martha Olsen Hochenauer, our mom, whose loving heart and creative spirit
showed us that peace is possible

George Hochenauer, our dad, who offered us an ever helpful hand and a sense
of Life's simplicity

We're grateful for . . .

The Spirit of life and love and for the goal of peace

Our partners, Terry Fox and Pat Monahan, for wholeheartedly embracing
us as well as our vision, and Terry for his untiring commitment to solving the
many puzzles of publishing

Our sister, Dr. Judy Hochenauer, a dedicated family therapist in Pasadena, CA,
whose laughter lifts our hearts

Ryan Gil de Montes for his expert technical and design assistance
TWP's Martha Oresman for her cheerful piloting

Our dear friends who support our bringing this story to young readers and
who continue sharing Life's fun and mysteries with us

And our esteemed felines, Sunny and Wondrous, Kitty Friend,
Portia and Beckett—for softening our lives!

The original
Sunny and Wondrous

Text copyright © 2006 by Mary Hochenauer and Lois (Suji) Hochenauer-Fox
Illustrations copyright © 2006 by Diane Lucas

Published by Gnatcatcher Children's Books • P.O. Box 18692 Long Beach, CA 90807
www.gnatcatcherpublishing.com

LCCN: 2006906514
First Edition
ISBN: 0-9778005-0-4

Printed and bound by Tien Wah Press in Singapore

Dear Reader,

Once upon a time
there were two cats named
Sunny and Wondrous.

Sunny lived with Claire near the ocean.
Wondrous lived with Ella in the country.

Claire and Ella were cousins—
and very good friends. So, naturally,
they wanted their cats, Sunny and Wondrous,
to become *very good cat-cousin friends.*

This story tells exactly how that happens,
one Thanksgiving Day!

We hope you enjoy it!
Your author friends,
Mary and Suji

"Come on, Sunny! It's Thanksgiving!" Claire called.
"We're going to my cousin Ella's. And *you're* going to meet
your cat cousin!"

"CAT COUSIN!" Sunny cried. "Oh! No! I want to play
with the sea gulls—I mean, *chase* them a little."

Hearing only "Meow," Claire continued. "Your cat
cousin's name is Wondrous. Now, Sunny, please get into your
cage. We're going to have so-o-o much fun!"

Ella and her family were also greeting the crisp Thanksgiving morning.

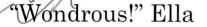

"Wondrous!" Ella called. "Claire's on her way with Sunny, your cat cousin! We hope you'll be best friends, just like Claire and me!"

"BEST FRIENDS!" cried Wondrous. "Oh! No! Now, I can't play with my new gnatcatcher! And I'm definitely not sharing it with any 'cat cousin'!"

Hearing only "Meow," Ella continued. "We're going to have so-o-o much fun! Oh, and, Wondrous," she called out, flying downstairs,

"you'd be a really good cat if you shared your stuff with Sunny."

A little later, Claire and Sunny arrived at Ella's.

"I don't want to wait in the garage," Sunny complained. "Well, at least, I'll be away from *Wondrous* for awhile."

Watching from the window, Wondrous said, "Thank goodness *Sunny's* not coming in yet."

The two cats pretended not to see each other.

By noon, the whole family had arrived and was sharing
Thanksgiving hugs and laughter. Spicy pumpkin! Roasted turkey!
Cranberries simmering in the pot!
Autumn's golden light filled this
happy afternoon.

Helping mash the potatoes, Ella and Claire exclaimed, "Our cats are going to be the best cat-cousin friends ever!"

Sunny and Wondrous still didn't like the idea . . .

. . . or did they?

Slipping away from the
Thanksgiving bustle,
Wondrous padded through the
warm kitchen and stood staring
at the door to the garage.

On the other side of the door, Sunny sat, cold and alone, among the rakes and shovels and mud-caked shoes.

Sniff.

Sniff, from the other side of the door.

"Meow," Wondrous called out bravely.

"Meow," Sunny answered, pressing his whiskers to the door.

"How are you doing out there?" Wondrous asked.

"Not very well," he said. "I'm not so sure about this cat-cousin plan."

Wondrous sighed. "Claire and Ella get some pretty crazy ideas. Last Friday, they tried to brush my teeth!"

"Eeew! Yesterday, they made *me* wear a soccer shirt!"

Both cats groaned.

"Dinnertime!"
Ella's mom
called to
everyone.
"Wondrous,
I have
something
for you—
and
for Sunny,
too,
of course."

"Gotta go," Wondrous said. "Um, Sunny, when
Claire and Ella bring you into the house today, would
you please not go looking for my things?"

She heard Sunny gulp.

"Well," she added quickly, "I guess I *could* let you
play with my green-striped mouse." Certainly not
my new gnatcatcher, she thought to herself, walking
towards the dining room and her bowl.

The family was gathered around the festive Thanksgiving table. Wondrous stopped to listen. She heard Grandpa say, "I'm thankful for my family and good health."

Auntie was saying, "With all the troubles in the world,
I pray that people
will choose
love over fear."

"Hmm," Wondrous thought. "Love over fear . . . ."

Then Claire said, "I'm grateful for Sunny! He's so smart and handsome." And Ella said, "I'm grateful for Wondrous. She's the sweetest kitty in the world."

Wondrous smiled. Then, she thought,
"The sweetest kitty in the world—*am* I?"

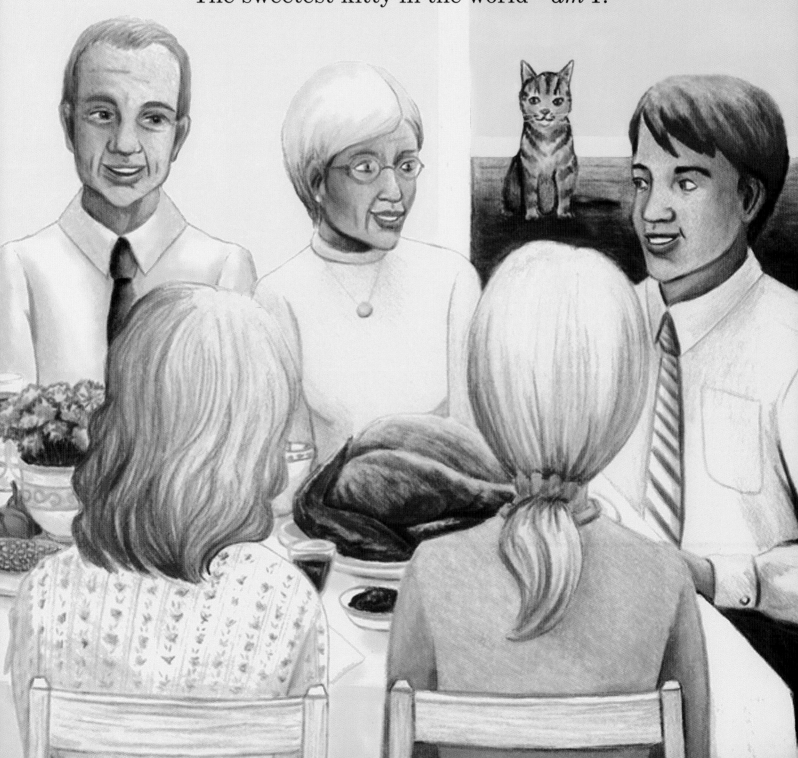

Wondrous walked to her dish where she found some juicy turkey. She was about to take a nibble when she paused—then scurried away.

Scratch.

Scratch, from the other side of the door.

"Sunny!" Wondrous whispered loudly. "I brought you something."

"What?" asked Sunny eagerly.

"Some turkey!" she answered. "And whipped cream for dessert! And, well—a blanket—in case you're cold out there."

"Gosh! What made you change your . . . ?"

Just then, Claire and Ella appeared. "At last we get to introduce our cats!" cried Claire. "Oh! Wondrous is already here! WHAT has she got in her paws?"

Ella smiled in surprise. Then, they opened the door to the garage.

Holding high her gifts for her cat cousin, Wondrous stepped eagerly into the garage.

Sunny, however, felt torn between his new friendship with Wondrous— and his freedom.

Sunny leapt for the safe glow of the kitchen!

At the same time,
Claire tripped on the blanket and sprawled over both cats,
one coming, one going.

Whipped cream spun into orbits.

Ella whirled through the whiteness,
tumbling onto Claire.

Wondrous turned and flew after the soaring Sunny!

Racing through the house,
the two cats flipped
Grandpa's chessboard,
scattered Auntie's saucers,
and toppled the tart tray!

In the hallway,
Sunny skidded to a halt
and turned gleefully to
face Wondrous. She
was not gleeful at all!

She hissed.

He hissed back.

She clawed.

He clawed back.

Fur raised and fur flew!
The two cat cousins
were locked in
an angry cat hug.

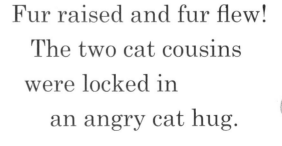

"Stop!" Claire and Ella shouted, rushing into the hallway, whipped cream dripping off their elbows.

"Meow! Reow! *You* spoiled everything!" Wondrous spat.

"Meow! Reow! *You* said I couldn't touch any of your stuff."

Ella scooped up Wondrous. Claire scooped up Sunny. They marched in opposite directions down the hall.

"I thought we could be friends," shrieked Wondrous over Ella's shoulder. "I brought you those nice things!"

"I was tired of waiting. I wanted to be inside, too!" wailed Sunny.

Claire set Sunny down in the study and closed the door. Ella set Wondrous down, warning her, "You behave!"

At bedtime, everyone headed upstairs.

All was quiet.

Sitting on the couch, Wondrous wondered how things had turned into such a muddle. "I'm sure Sunny didn't want to be mean to me," she thought. "He's probably a perfectly nice cat."

In the study, Sunny lay on the carpet pondering. "I think I hurt Wondrous' feelings. She came to visit me twice and even brought me presents!"

Sunny crept to the door. "Wondrous," he called softly.

Already at the door, Wondrous slid her paw under it. It swung open! The two cats stood face to face.

"Um," Wondrous said finally. "I felt scared— that you wouldn't like me."

Giving her a shy look, Sunny said, "I felt scared, too—that you wouldn't like me, either."

Slowly, the two cats moved, one paw closer to each other.

"I'm sorry for not wanting to share my toys with you," Wondrous said.

"I'm sorry for running away from you," Sunny said.

"Thank you," they both whispered. "Let's be friends."

"Okay!"

The two cats jumped up and scampered
through the moonlit house, stopping to nibble turkey
and lick whipped cream.

They played. They wrestled.
And they nipped
each other's ears.

Finally, at dawn,
they sank,
breathless,
onto soft pillows.

"Do you think *all* cats can have this much fun?" Sunny asked.

Wondrous suddenly remembered Auntie's dinner-table words. "They can—
if they choose love
over fear."

"What do you mean,
'love over fear'?"

"I mean, when
you and I were feeling
fear and anger, what we really wanted to feel—was *love!*"

"So," Sunny squealed, "we shared our feelings and said we were sorry! *Then,* we felt love!"

"Yes!" Wondrous replied happily. "And then,
we got to play and have fun!"

"So, if *we* can do it—*any* cat can do it!" they both purred.

A moment later, Wondrous asked, "Sunny, do you think *PEOPLE* can have this much fun?"

"Of course they can—*if they choose love over fear!*"

Next morning, coming downstairs, Ella sighed and said, "I guess Sunny and Wondrous aren't going to be friends, after all."

"You're probably right," Claire agreed sadly.

The two cousins headed into the breakfast room
for the surprise of their lives.

There, in a puddle of early-morning sunlight,
two *very good cat-cousin friends* lay sleeping peacefully,
the toy gnatcatcher resting between them.

Dear Parents and Teachers,

This story shows how we all can choose to live in harmony by telling the truth about our feelings and apologizing for our mistakes. As you read with your children, you might ask them some questions:

- *How do you know when you're having a problem?* (I feel scared. I feel mad. I worry. I yell. My heart pounds. I don't know what to do.)

- *What are some things you can do when you're having a problem?* (I can get quiet and think about it. I can take a deep breath. I can talk to an adult about my problem. I can talk with the person with whom I'm having the problem and listen to them. I can tell them how I feel and what I want. I can say I'm sorry.)

- *How did Sunny and Wondrous solve their problem?*
(Discuss this with your children when you finish reading the story.)

We hope you and your children will enjoy our story and that your discussions about peaceful conflict resolution will reap satisfying results.

Sincerely,

Mary and Suji

About the Authors

Mary Hochenauer and Lois (Suji) Hochenauer-Fox write books for young people and teach adolescents in public schools. Aware of the world's crucial need to solve conflicts non-violently, the two sisters show their students how to resolve daily conflicts honestly, fairly and peaceably. As for very young readers, characters Sunny and Wondrous demonstrate just how rewarding this practice can be!

Suji and Mary also like to travel, sing and garden. Fresh from a sailing adventure in Tonga, Mary plays tennis and performs in a community chorale. Suji, a former personal growth counselor, practices yoga and writes and performs her songs. When working together on a book, the sisters often delight in such backyard miracles as two quail and a rabbbit sipping from the same puddle.

Mary's real-life Sunny lives with her at the beach while Suji's cat Wondrous lives with her in the country. The two felines did meet one Thanksgiving, but unlike their character counterparts, they didn't practice peaceful conflict resolution. *We humans can learn to do better!*

About the Illustrator

Diane Lucas is an artist and illustrator with a Bachelor of Fine Arts from the University of Victoria. She has illustrated numerous book covers and picture books. Diane lives in Nova Scotia, Canada with her husband, two children, and three cats. Her work may be viewed at www.lucasillustration.com.

About the Gnatcatcher

The California gnatcatcher is an endangered blue-gray bird that lives in the protected hills around Suji's home in Southern California. Suji's cat, Wondrous, has become content to live indoors in order to do her part in preserving this species of small birds. And Sunny doesn't really chase seagulls at the beach, either, because Mary won't let him, and, well, because he doesn't like sand.

What People Are Saying

". . . an excellent tool to help students build healthy relationships through listening and honest sharing—just the thing for a child who's feeling unsure or struggling with family or peer relationships." —Ginny Bohn, Elementary and Special Education Teacher

". . . a beautiful story, easily used in the home, classroom or therapeutic setting. It illustrates how well the principle of love over fear works to bring us all closer together." —Ann M. Bingham Newman, Ph.D., CSULA, MFCT, Child Therapist

". . . a charming story of cat characters who discover the power of choosing love over fear when they disclose feelings and listen to each other with compassion." —Tim Ryan, Ph.D., D. Div., Certified NLP Trainer, Marriage and Family Counselor